TROLL
TREASURY OF
ANIMAL
STORIES

Library of Congress Cataloging-in-Publication Data

Troll treasury of animal stories / edited by John C. Miles;
    illustrated by Mary Oak-Rhind and Graham Dennison.
        p.   cm.
        Summary: Forty-five traditional stories about animals.
        ISBN 0-8167-2240-4 (lib. bdg.)   ISBN 0-8167-2241-2 (pbk.)
        1. Tales. [1. Animals—Folklore.   2. Folklore.]   I. Miles, John
C., 1960-   .   II. Oak-Rhind, Mary, ill.   III. Dennison, Graham,
ill.   IV. Troll Associates.   V. Title: Treasury of Animal stories.
PZ8.1.T7385   1991
398.24'5—dc20   90-11158

Published in the U.S.A. by Troll Associates, Inc.,
100 Corporate Drive, Mahwah, New Jersey.
Produced for Troll Associates, Inc., by
Joshua Morris Publishing Inc. in association
with Harper Collins.
Copyright © 1991 by Harper Collins.
Printed in Belgium.
10 9 8 7 6 5 4 3 2 1

TROLL
TREASURY OF
ANIMAL
STORIES

Edited by John C. Miles
Illustrated by Mary Oak–Rhind
and Graham Dennison

Troll Associates

Contents

The Flying Tortoise

A tortoise grew very tired of spending his life on the ground with a shell on his back. All the other animals seemed much freer to move around. Birds even flew in the air. The tortoise wanted to be a bird most of all.

One day, a friendly eagle flew down beside the tortoise and began to talk to him. "What a safe and steady life you lead," said the eagle. "I wish I was like you. You don't have to be afraid of anything. You are safe inside your house of shell."

"Alas," said the tortoise with a sigh, "it's a very dull life for me. There is no change. Day in, day out, I crawl around in the mud. Now, *you* are a king of the air. If I could fly, I would be the happiest animal on the earth. Will you please teach me how it's done?"

"You can't fly!" protested the eagle. "And you'd be much better off staying on the ground."

So the eagle picked the tortoise up in his talons and flew into the air with him. When they had flown higher than the highest hill, the eagle said, "I have done my part. I'll now leave you to do the rest."

"Thanks," said the tortoise. "Let me go, and you'll see how easily I can fly."

The eagle let go, and the tortoise fell toward the ground.

"Help!" cried the terrified tortoise, plummeting.

The eagle swooped quickly down and caught him just in time. "I hope you'll be happy from now on," said the eagle. "You just can't change nature, and it's no good trying."

Thanking the eagle, the tortoise waddled off. He was glad to be back on the ground again.

"I'm tired of the ground," grumbled the tortoise. "Show me how to fly!" He begged and begged so hard that at last the eagle said he would do his best.

"I can take you up into the air," said the eagle, "and then let you try it for yourself. But you'll be sorry that you ever left the ground."

"No, I won't!" said the tortoise. "I'll fly like a bird and be as happy as can be."

The Dog
And the Rooster

Once upon a time, a dog and a rooster set out on a trip together to see the world. They wandered about very happily on the first day. By the time night fell, they had reached a forest.

"We had better spend the night here," said the dog. "This hollow tree will make a good resting place for both of us. You can roost on a branch. I'll curl up inside the bottom of this hollow trunk."

So the rooster flew up to one of the branches, and the dog settled down to sleep inside the base of the tree.

The rooster woke early in the morning as usual. He flapped his wings and began to crow.

This attracted the attention of a hungry fox. The fox was returning

from an unsuccessful raid on a farmyard. He stopped beneath the tree and looked up at the rooster. "What a wonderful breakfast that rooster would make," the fox said to himself, licking his lips, "if only I could get him down."

The rooster crowed on and didn't pay any attention to the hungry fox below.

After a little while, the fox spoke to him. "Good morning, Mr. Rooster," he said. "You have the finest voice I have ever heard. Won't you come down and sing to me so that I can hear you better?"

"No thanks," said the rooster. "I can sing better up here."

"Please come down," pleaded the fox. "Just for me."

"If you really want me to come down," said the rooster, "you have to ask the doorman below to open the door."

So the fox, who was almost sure of his breakfast by now, looked into the hollow of the tree to wake up the doorman. To his surprise and terror, out dashed the dog, who chased him out of the forest.

The rooster crowed on happily, and the fox went home hungrier than ever.

The Straw Ox

The old man and the old woman, both very poor, lived on a farm. They had few farm animals, and their crops were small and scrawny.

One day, the old woman had an idea. "Husband," she said, "make me a straw ox and smear it with tar."

"Why, you foolish woman!" said the old man. "What's the use of an ox like that?"

"Never mind," she said.

So her husband made the ox of straw, and he smeared it all over with tar.

Early the next morning, the old woman drove the straw ox out into the field to graze. She sat down nearby and soon was fast asleep.

While she was dozing, a bear came rushing out upon the ox.

The bear said, "Who are you? Speak and tell me!"

And the ox said, "I am an ox, stuffed with straw and covered with tar."

"Oh!" said the bear. "Stuffed with straw and covered with tar, are you? Then give me some of your straw and tar that I may patch up my ragged fur!"

"Take some," said the ox.

The bear buried his teeth in the tar until he found he couldn't let go again. He tugged and he tugged, but it was no use.

The old woman awoke and saw what had happened. She called to her husband, "Look, look! The ox has brought us a bear!" The old man ran out, captured the bear, and put him in the cellar.

The next morning, the old woman again drove the ox into the field to graze. She sat down

10

nearby and soon fell asleep.

While she dozed, a gray wolf came rushing out upon the ox and said, "Who are you? Tell me!"

"I am an ox, stuffed with straw and covered with tar," said the ox.

"Oh! Stuffed with straw and covered with tar, are you? Then give me some of your tar to patch up my ragged fur!"

"Take some," said the ox.

The wolf bit into the tar. He tried to let go but couldn't.

When the old woman awoke, she saw what had happened. She ran and told her husband, who came and threw the wolf into the cellar with the bear.

On the third day, the old woman again drove the ox into the pasture to graze. She sat down nearby and dozed off.

A fox happened to stray into the field. "Who are you?" he said to the ox.

The ox answered in the same way, and soon the fox was in the cellar with the bear and the wolf.

Then the old man went down to the cellar and began sharpening a knife. The bear said to him, "Tell me, why are you sharpening your knife?"

"To make a coat for myself out of your heavy fur."

"Oh, don't! Let me go, and I'll bring you a lot of honey."

"Very well," said the old man, and he let the bear go.

Then he began sharpening his knife again. The wolf asked him,

"What are you sharpening your knife for?"

"To make a warm fur hat against the winter cold."

"Oh, don't! Let me go, and I'll bring you a whole herd of sheep."

"Well, make sure you do!" said the old man, and he let the wolf go.

Then he sat down and began sharpening his knife again. The fox asked him, "Be so kind and tell me, why are you sharpening your knife?"

"From your fur," said the old man, "I can make wonderful gloves and mittens."

"Oh, please don't. Let me go, and I will bring you hens and geese."

"Very well, but see that you do it!" The old man let the fox go.

Early the next morning, there was a noise in the doorway. The old man went out, and there was the bear carrying a whole hive full of honey. And there was the wolf driving a whole flock of sheep into the courtyard. Behind the wolf came the fox, driving before him geese and hens.

The old man sold the geese at the market. When he returned home, his wife was making coats, hats, gloves, and mittens out of wool clipped from the sheep. After she finished, the two sat down to a delicious meal of honey and eggs.

The old man and the old woman felt poor no more — thanks to the straw ox.

The Magic Cow

Once upon a time in Ireland, there were some elves called leprechauns who lived in a lake. Every evening, they would lead their herd of magic cows out of the lake and into a field to graze.

But one evening, one of the magic cows wandered away. She joined a nearby herd of brown cows belonging to a farmer named Patrick.

The next morning, Patrick came out to call his cows for milking. He was delighted to find a magic cow there. "Now I will get rich!" he said.

Sure enough, the magic cow gave richer, creamier milk than any of the other cows. Everybody wanted to buy Patrick's special milk and cream. They were the best around.

Time passed on, and the magic cow had calves. When those calves grew into cows, they had calves of their own. Patrick now had a large herd of cattle. Many of them had magic cow blood in their veins. These cows all produced rich, creamy milk, just like the first magic cow. Patrick became very rich.

The magic cow was getting very old. She gave less and less milk. Patrick decided to fatten her up and sell her to the butcher. Patrick's wife warned him not to be so foolish. But Patrick had grown greedy as well as rich, and he would not listen.

The day came when Patrick decided the magic cow should be killed. The butcher came to Patrick's farm. All the neighbors came to watch.

The butcher raised his ax. But before he could strike, there was a loud cry. Everybody turned. There, standing beside the lake, was one of the leprechauns.

"Come, magic cow," he called. "Come home."

The magic cow lifted her head and listened. Then, before anyone could stop her, she ran toward the lake. After her ran her children, her grandchildren, and her great-grandchildren.

Patrick and his neighbors ran after the cows. But they were too late. They watched as the magic cow and the rest of Patrick's herd plunged into the water.

None of the cows was ever seen again. But on the spot where each cow had disappeared, a milky white water lily flowered for ever after.

13

The Farmer And the Eagle

Early one morning, a farmer took his hayfork and headed out to work in his hayfield. The field was just outside the walls of the city where the farmer lived.

On his way to the field, the farmer heard a strange noise coming from behind some bushes. It sounded like the flapping of enormous wings. The farmer looked around the bushes and stared in amazement. There, with one talon caught in a rabbit snare, was a magnificent eagle.

The farmer gazed at the eagle's fierce hooked beak, piercing eyes, and mighty wings. He wondered what to do. A shepherd would have said, "Kill the eagle, or leave it there to starve. Otherwise, it will take my lambs."

But the farmer could not allow such a beautiful creature to die. Speaking softly, he approached the eagle. Holding one arm up to his face for protection, the farmer released the snare and set the bird free.

He watched with pleasure as the eagle flew off with a great beat of its wings. Then the farmer picked up his hayfork and went on his way.

All morning long, the farmer

worked hard. By lunchtime, he was hot and tired. He sat down to rest against the old stones of the city wall. Soon he fell asleep.

A few minutes later, he woke up, aware that something had touched him. Then he realized what had happened. An eagle had swooped down and snatched the cap from his head. It now flew just out of reach, with the cap dangling from its talons.

The farmer jumped to his feet. He tried to grab the cap, but the eagle kept just ahead of him. When the farmer was in the middle of the field, the eagle dropped the cap.

As the farmer bent to pick up his cap, there was a loud, rumbling, crashing noise. Turning around, he saw that a huge stone had fallen from the city wall. The stone landed on the exact spot where he had been sleeping. If the farmer had stayed sleeping there, he would have been killed.

The farmer looked up in amazement at the eagle soaring high in the sky. It was the same bird he had released from the trap earlier that day. Just as the farmer had saved the eagle's life, the eagle had returned to save the farmer.

The Dog And the Bone

Once there was a dog who liked to hang around the back door of a butcher's shop. She hoped someone would throw her a bone. Whenever she saw the butcher, she would gaze up longingly at him and whine. But he always said, "No meat for mutts! Get lost! Scram!"

Then a young boy came to help the butcher. He loved dogs. He would often toss bits of meat to her when the butcher was not looking. The dog would gobble them up before other dogs saw what she had and tried to snatch them away from her.

Soon other dogs found out about the young boy. They also came to beg. The boy fed all of them, but he still saved the best bones for the first dog.

"This one is for you, Beauty," he would say.

One day, there was a big ham bone in the butcher's shop. The boy hid it until he could take it outside to Beauty.

The other dogs began to growl and grumble. They also wanted the bone for themselves. They chased Beauty for a while, then gave up.

Beauty headed for the woods beyond the town. She could eat her bone in peace there. She stopped by a stream. To see if it looked like a good place to drink, she peered down into the water. What she saw made her jump with surprise. There, in the water, was another dog. The dog had a bone that looked bigger than hers. That rotten boy at the butcher's must have found another favorite dog. He gave the other dog the best bone of all. She'd soon fix that!

With an angry snarl, the dog dropped her own bone. She reached forward to snatch the other one. But the water became full of ripples, and she could no longer see the bone.

Too late, she realized her mistake. She was staring at her own reflection. She had dropped her lovely bone into the stream. Now she had nothing. Feeling rather foolish, the dog went back to the town.

"Hi there, Beauty!" cried the boy. "Back already? No more bones, I'm afraid, but you can have this little pork scrap."

The dog wagged her tail gratefully. From now on, she decided, she would be happy with whatever she was given.

Why the Bear Is Stumpy-Tailed

Long ago on a winter afternoon, a bear met an old fox who was carrying a string of fish on his back.

"My," said the bear, "where did you get such a fine string of fish?"

Now the fox was as sly as sly could be. He didn't want the bear to know that he hadn't caught the fish himself.

"Ha!" the fox said with a sly smile. "I caught them myself! I caught them just a little while ago. And I'm thinking how good they will taste for supper. Why don't you catch some, too?"

The bear was getting hungry, so he wanted some fish right away. "What's the best way to catch them?" he asked.

The sly fox said, "Go down to the river and cut a hole in the ice. Then put your long tail in the hole and wait for the fish to bite.

"When the fish bite your tail, it may hurt a little. But to catch a lot of fish, you must sit there as long as you can.

"The longer you sit and keep your tail in the river, the more fish you'll catch. When you think you have caught enough, pull out your tail. Now remember what I've told you."

"Thanks, Brother Fox," said the bear. "It's a strange way to catch fish. But I'll do it, and I do hope the fish will bite."

"Hee-hee," giggled the sly old fox, as the bear ran toward the river.

18

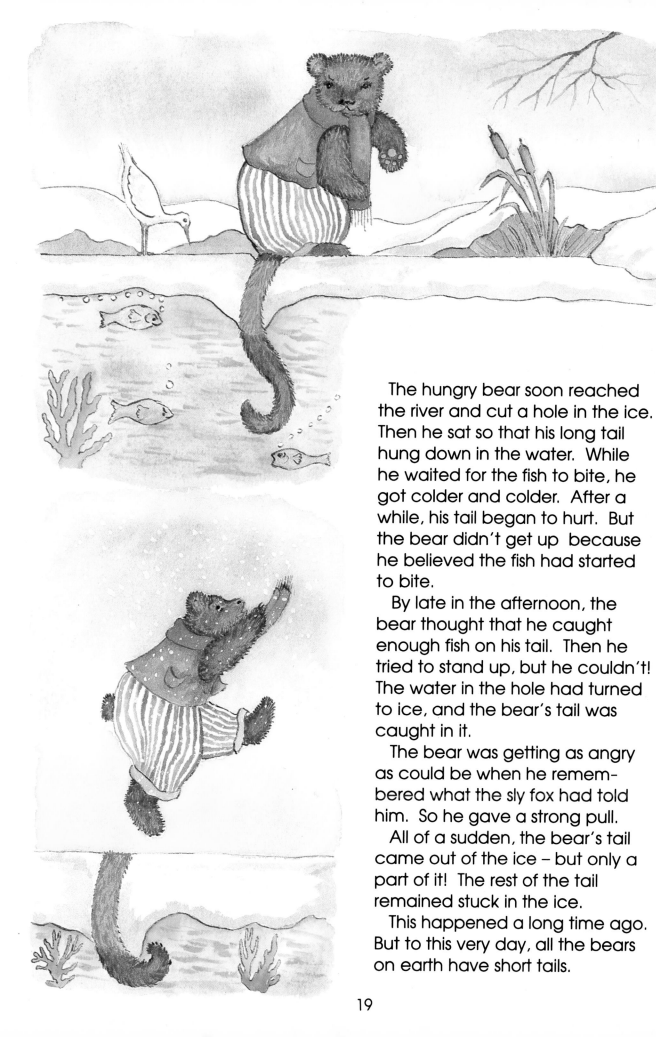

The hungry bear soon reached the river and cut a hole in the ice. Then he sat so that his long tail hung down in the water. While he waited for the fish to bite, he got colder and colder. After a while, his tail began to hurt. But the bear didn't get up because he believed the fish had started to bite.

By late in the afternoon, the bear thought that he caught enough fish on his tail. Then he tried to stand up, but he couldn't! The water in the hole had turned to ice, and the bear's tail was caught in it.

The bear was getting as angry as could be when he remembered what the sly fox had told him. So he gave a strong pull.

All of a sudden, the bear's tail came out of the ice – but only a part of it! The rest of the tail remained stuck in the ice.

This happened a long time ago. But to this very day, all the bears on earth have short tails.

Johnny Appleseed And the Mother Bear

There once lived a boy named John Chapman. Wearing a red and white handkerchief around his neck, John used to go out into the countryside. There, he would spend hours looking at the birds, flowers, and his favorite tree of all, the apple tree.

John thought that everyone should have the chance to enjoy the beauty of apple trees and taste their delicious fruit. So when he grew up, he set off with a sack of apple seeds that he planted all over America. He became known as Johnny Appleseed.

Every year, when planting time was over, Johnny would build himself a shelter for the long winter. Then, all kinds of animals would come to him — foxes, wolves, deer. Even the bears knew he would not hurt them, and they kept him company. Johnny fed them with his own supply of nuts and berries. The animals never forgot his kindness.

In the spring, he would leave his shelter and tend his apple trees. Then fall would come again, and he would plant more apple seeds.

One winter, Johnny caught a bad cold. He was tossing and turning on his bed in his shelter. He was too weak to go and find help or even to make himself a meal.

On the third day of his illness, a mother bear and her cub came by the shelter to visit Johnny.

They pushed open the door and saw him lying there. They stepped around him carefully and sniffed him for a while.

The mother bear gently nudged Johnny to try and wake him up. But it was no use. The bears finally walked off. Held between the mother bear's teeth was the red and white handkerchief that Johnny always wore around his neck.

Two Indians out hunting saw the bears and the handkerchief between the mother's teeth. One Indian said to the other, "The bears have been to Johnny Appleseed's shelter. Perhaps they have killed him."

"No, no," said his companion. "Johnny Appleseed is a friend of the animals. They wouldn't hurt him. Something must be wrong."

The two Indians followed the bears' tracks. Soon they found themselves at Johnny's shelter. They could see that he was very ill. They would have to act quickly to save him.

The Indians wrapped Johnny in some blankets, carried him to their horses, and took him to their home. There, they gave him their medicines and fed him until he was well.

When Johnny Appleseed was ready to leave, he thanked the two Indians for saving his life.

"Do not thank us," said one of the Indians. "It was the mother bear who saved your life. The red and white handkerchief she held between her teeth warned us that something was wrong. She has repaid you for your kindness to our brothers, the animals."

The Fox
And the Crow

Once upon a time, a hungry fox went to look for some food. He went looking for it in a forest, where he saw a large crow sitting in a tree. The crow had a large piece of meat held in his beak.

"Ah!" said the fox to himself. "That looks good! My mouth is watering. I must try to get the meat from the crow."

He stopped underneath the tree and started to think. Then the fox began to flatter the crow.

"What a fine bird you are!" he said, pretending to admire the crow. "You are so graceful, and your feathers are so glossy. I think you're the most beautiful bird in the world!"

The crow seemed very pleased with this flattery. But he still held on to his food.

"If you only had a voice to suit the rest of your fine qualities," said the fox slyly, "surely there would be no more wonderful creature in the world! What kind of voice would it be? It would certainly be beautiful. Would it sound like a rippling brook in spring? Or would it sound like wind in the trees?"

The crow was very vain. He thought he already had a beautiful voice. And he wanted to show the fox just how beautiful it was. But he still had a large piece of meat in his beak. So finally the crow opened his beak wide and gave a loud squawk.

The piece of meat fell out of the crow's mouth. It fell straight down — into the fox's open mouth.

"You stupid bird!" he said between chews to the unhappy crow. "I may have said nice things about your looks, but there is nothing I can say in praise of your brains!"

A Dollar a Minute

One spring, Br'er Fox said to himself that he should plant a peanut patch. In a single day, he dug up a garden and planted the peanuts. He built a sturdy fence around the garden. Br'er Rabbit sat by and watched him.

When the peanuts began to grow and ripen, Br'er Fox went to inspect his patch. He found that somebody had been crawling around among the vines. Br'er Fox got mighty mad. He suspected Br'er Rabbit of stealing his peanuts.

Br'er Fox looked around his garden and soon spotted a hole in the fence. Right then and there, he set a trap. Br'er Fox bent down a tree, tied one end of a rope to it, and made a loop knot at the other end of the rope. Then he set the loop knot in such a way that anything coming through the fence hole would be caught and pulled up into the air.

The next morning, old Br'er Rabbit came hopping along and slipped through the fence hole. The loop knot caught his back legs, and the tree flew up into the air. There Br'er Rabbit swung upside down, wondering what would happen next.

While he was thinking up a tale to tell Br'er Fox, Br'er Rabbit heard a rumbling from somewhere down the road. Soon old Br'er Bear came lumbering along.

"Howdy, Br'er Bear!" said Br'er Rabbit, hanging in the air.

Br'er Bear looked all around. He didn't see anyone. Finally he looked up and saw Br'er Rabbit swinging from the tree. Br'er Bear yelled, "Hey, Br'er Rabbit! How do you feel this morning?"

"I'm okay, Br'er Bear," said Br'er Rabbit.

"What are you doing up there?" asked Br'er Bear.

Br'er Rabbit thought a moment, then said, "Why, I'm making a dollar a minute!"

"How?" asked Br'er Bear.

"I'm keeping crows out of Br'er Fox's peanut patch. Wouldn't you like to make a dollar a minute, Br'er Bear? I know you have a big family to take care of at home. Besides, you would make such a fine scarecrow."

Br'er Bear said that he would like the job. Br'er Rabbit told him how to bend down the tree. Before long, Br'er Bear was swinging up from the treetop in Br'er Rabbit's place.

As soon as he was free, Br'er Rabbit raced for Br'er Fox's house. When he got there, Br'er Rabbit called out, "Oh, Br'er Fox, come out! I'll show you the one who's been stealing your peanuts!"

Br'er Fox and Br'er Rabbit went running down to the peanut patch. When they got there, sure enough, there was old Br'er Bear.

"Now I've got you!" said Br'er Fox.

"Yes," said Br'er Rabbit. "You've got him all right, Br'er Fox!"

Br'er Bear looked confused. "When will I be paid?"

"Paid!" blurted Br'er Fox angrily. "Do you think I'm going to pay you for taking my peanuts?"

Before Br'er Bear had a chance to answer, Br'er Fox went home. He left Br'er Bear swinging from the tree all day long.

As for Br'er Rabbit, he ran off as fast as his legs could carry him. Never again did he enter Br'er Fox's peanut patch — nor did Br'er Bear.

The Crow
And the Pigeons

There was once a lazy crow who was always hungry. He thought it was too much trouble to look for food.

"Caw! Caw!" he said. "If only I had someone to bring me my food every day, how happy I'd be!"

One day, he saw a fat pigeon flying by.

"How happy and well fed it looks," the crow said to himself. "I'll follow it and see where it lives and how it finds food."

So the crow flew after the pigeon until they came to a park. The pigeon joined some other pigeons.

Before long, an old man came along and brought them a large bag of bread crusts. These made a good, full meal.

"Caw! Caw! No wonder they look so happy and fat," said the crow. "I'll wait until the man goes away, then I'll join them."

When the man had gone, the crow flew over to the pigeons. "Caw! Caw!" said he. "Can I share your food?"

"No, you can't!" shouted the pigeons, making a lot of noise and flying at him. "We want no strangers here." And they flew after him, pecking at him and chasing him away.

The crow went home feeling sad. But he made up his mind that somehow he would go and live with the pigeons. He wanted to be as well fed as they were.

At last, the crow had an idea. "I will paint my feathers gray," he said, "and then the pigeons will think I am one of them."

So the crow flew around until at last he found a can of gray paint that had been left lying outside a door. "This will suit me just fine," he said.

The crow took a bath in the paint until all his feathers were gray. "Now I look like a real pigeon," he said, very happy with himself.

He flew off to the park and found it empty. So he hopped around like a pigeon. Soon the other pigeons came back and welcomed him as one of the flock.

"It soon will be food time," said one of the pigeons.

"Good! I'm really hungry," said the crow, trying to remember not to give himself away by saying "Caw!"

Just then, the old man came to give the pigeons their food. It looked so good and the crow was so hungry that he got very excited. He yelled out, "Caw! Caw! Give lots to me! Caw! Caw!"

Suddenly, the pigeons turned on him. They pecked at him so badly that he had to fly away before he could taste any food.

Sadly, the crow flew home to his own forest. But when his old friends, the other crows, saw him, they immediately chased him away. They did not recognize him because of his gray-painted feathers.

"Go back to your own home," they shouted. "We don't want strangers here."

So the crow found himself worse off than ever. His own friends would have nothing to do with him, and the pigeons would not let him into their flock.

"What looks easier isn't always so," the crow said to himself. "I wish I had never painted my feathers gray!"

The Crow
And the Mussel

Once upon a time, a greedy crow flew to the beach to look for food. At last, he saw a kind of clam called a mussel lying on the sand. He knew that inside the shell he would find a nice meal. So he started to try and break open the shell.

The crow pecked at it with his beak and battered it against a stone. But the shell would not break. He was getting hungrier and hungrier – and angrier and angrier.

About this time, another crow flew in. He landed a few feet away. He watched the other crow trying to break open the shell.

"Friend crow," he said, "I have an idea that will get you the meal you want. Pick up the mussel in your beak and fly as high as you can. Then drop the mussel against a rock. You will find that it will break open, and you will have your meal."

"Good idea!" said the first crow. At once, he picked up the mussel and flew away.

28

The second crow waited patiently on the beach. Soon the mussel came falling down out of the sky. The shell smashed to bits on a large stone. The second crow swooped toward it and ate up the tasty meat before the other crow could reach it.

"You ate my food!" said the first crow after flying back down.

"If you hadn't been so greedy," said the second crow, "you would have taken a few minutes and thought up a plan as quickly as I did. If you had, you'd have your meal by now. As it is, I thought up the plan, so I should get the food." And with that, the second crow flew away.

The Meeting Of the Mice

A group of mice once lived together in an old house. There were plenty of holes where they could hide, and food was easy to find. They had a good time together. The mice would have been perfectly happy if it had not been for a big, mean cat who also lived in the house.

This cat was very fierce. She liked to chase mice all the time. Day and night, she chased after them, snapping at their tails, eagerly trying to catch them.

No sooner did the mice come out of their holes than a mouse was sure to shout, "Help! Here comes the cat!" Then the mice had to run for their lives and hide again.

The situation became so bad that the mice decided to hold a meeting to try to solve the problem.

"What can we do?" asked the head mouse, trying not to lose hope. "My best friend almost got caught last week, and my aunt the week before. We can't go on like this. Soon there may not be any of us left! We've got to teach that horrible cat a lesson she won't forget in a hurry."

"But how?" asked some of the others.

"Why not set a trap?" one mouse suggested. "We could dig a hole and cover it with leaves."

"How could we do that?" said the head mouse. "We could never dig a hole big enough for a cat. No, we must think of something else."

"If only we could think of some way of being warned when the cat is on the prowl," said another

mouse. "Then we'd have time to run away and hide safely before we're chased."

All the mice sat thinking for a long time.

Suddenly, a young mouse jumped to his feet. "I have it!" he cried. "Let's put a bell around the cat's neck. It will jingle every time she walks, and we will hear her coming before it's too late."

"Great idea!" said the head mouse. "That's wonderful. You are a very smart mouse. This is the idea that will save us!"

The young mouse sat down, while everybody else cheered loudly. He looked very happy with himself. All around him other mice were congratulating him.

While this was going on, a very old mouse, who had kept his mouth shut until then, slowly stood up and cleared his throat. The other mice stopped talking.

"Good friends," he said, "I have no doubt that this is a very good idea. But who's going to volunteer to hang the bell on the cat?"

The other mice looked at each other in dismay.

"Not me," said one or two.

"Nope!" whispered another.

Not one mouse was willing to go near the cat to hang a bell around her neck. So in the end, the wonderful idea didn't work. Nobody had thought all the way through the plan.

Br'er Fox Invites Br'er Rabbit to Dinner

One day, Br'er Fox had been doing all that he could to catch Br'er Rabbit. And Br'er Rabbit had been doing all that he could to keep Br'er Fox from catching him. After great effort, Br'er Fox was no closer to his goal than when he started. That's when he decided to have a little game with Br'er Rabbit.

When Br'er Rabbit came hopping down the road late that same afternoon, Br'er Fox called out to him. "Hold on there, Br'er Rabbit. I saw Br'er Bear yesterday. He scolded me because we can't live peacefully like good neighbors. I told him I'd try to patch things up with you."

Br'er Rabbit scratched behind one ear and thought a minute. "All right, Br'er Fox," he replied. "Why don't you come over to my house tomorrow and have dinner with me? We don't have anything fancy, but I expect we can make something for you."

"I'd like that," said Br'er Fox.

The next day, Mr. and Mrs. Rabbit raided a vegetable garden and brought home some cabbages, corn, and asparagus. They fixed up a delicious dinner. Soon one of the little Rabbits came running in the house and shouted, "Oh, Pa! I saw Mr. Fox coming!"

Br'er Rabbit and his family waited and waited, but Br'er Fox never came. After a while, Br'er Rabbit went to the door and peeked out. There, sticking out from behind the house, was the tip of Br'er Fox's tail. Br'er Rabbit knew that Br'er Fox was up to something, so he just shut the door and had dinner without Br'er Fox.

The next day, Br'er Fox sent a message to Br'er Rabbit. He said he was sorry he hadn't come to dinner, but he had been very sick. He asked Br'er Rabbit to come and have dinner at his house. Br'er Rabbit decided to go.

When Br'er Rabbit got there, he heard somebody groaning. He looked in the door and saw Br'er Fox sitting in a rocking chair. He was wrapped up in a blanket and looked very weak. Br'er Rabbit looked all around, but he didn't see any dinner.

"What's for dinner, Br'er Fox?" asked Br'er Rabbit with a knowing smile.

"Why, uh, chicken," answered Br'er Fox uneasily.

Br'er Rabbit stroked his long whiskers and said, "Do you have any calamus root? I can't eat chicken if it's not seasoned with calamus root. I'll just hop out and get some."

Br'er Rabbit backed out of the door. Then he hopped down the road and jumped behind some calamus plants. He sat there watching for Br'er Fox.

Br'er Rabbit didn't have to watch for long. A very healthy-looking Br'er Fox ran out of the house and started to look for Br'er Rabbit. Then Br'er Rabbit shouted out, "Oh, Br'er Fox! Here's some calamus root for you. I'll just leave it on a tree stump." And with that, Br'er Rabbit merrily dashed home.

Br'er Fox hasn't caught Br'er Rabbit yet. And with Br'er Rabbit's quick wits, he probably never will!

The Geese That Saved Rome

Once there was an Italian farmer who had a fine flock of geese. The geese made excellent guardians. If any robbers or wolves came near, they honked in alarm. A wise old gander led the flock. His favorite saying was "All roads lead to Rome."

One year, the old farmer died. A stranger bought the farm. The geese did not like him, so they held a meeting to decide what to do. One clever young gosling said, "Let's follow the road to Rome, as Grandpa Gander always told us to do."

All the geese, who now numbered twelve, set off on the long walk to Rome. Some were lost on the way. Some were carried off by foxes. Only four geese reached Rome.

The survivors found themselves struggling in the large crowds. Then one goose was captured by a fat man, who tucked her under his arm with a loud laugh. The remaining three gazed sadly after her.

"She'll be eaten for dinner," said one.

They all sat down feeling very unhappy. Then they noticed the crowd around them was standing back to allow a group of men to pass. They were heading for a huge temple on the hill.

"Let's follow them," said one goose. Up the hill they waddled. The people stared at the three geese and tried to grab them.

34

But the leader of the group of men saw them and said, "Let them stay. They may be here for a good reason."

One day, an enemy army invaded Rome. The city was captured except for the hill where all the Roman people fled. The enemy decided to attack the hill at night.

Silently, they climbed up the steep hillside. They had nearly reached the top when one soldier slipped and fell with a cry. The geese woke up and honked furiously. The Roman guards were startled awake. They drove the enemy off just in time. Rome was saved.

The Romans were very grateful to the three geese. They placed golden chains around their necks. The road to Rome had led the geese to success after all.

Little Half Chick

Once upon a time in Spain, a black hen had a brood of chicks. The last one to hatch had only one leg, one wing, one eye, and half a tail. Everyone called him Little Half Chick, for that was what he was.

As he was growing up, Little Half Chick was often very rude. He always wanted his own way. One day, he hopped up to his mother on one leg. He announced, "I am going to Madrid to see the king." And away he hopped.

On the way, he came to a stream that was choked with weeds. "Little Half Chick!" called the stream. "Please pull out some of the weeds. Then I can flow freely to meet the river."

"Not me!" he replied. "I'm off to Madrid to see the king." And away he hopped.

Soon he came to a very weak fire. It was about to go out. "Little Half Chick!" called the fire. "Please get me some sticks or dry leaves, or I will die!"

"Not me!" he replied. "I'm off to Madrid to see the king." And away he hopped.

The next day, he passed a big chestnut tree. He heard a sad moaning in the branches. It was the wind, caught in the leaves. "Little Half Chick!" called the wind. "Please pull me free!"

"Not me!" said Little Half Chick. "I'm off to Madrid to see the king." And away he hopped.

Soon Little Half Chick entered

the city of Madrid. He came to a beautiful palace. At that moment, a kitchen maid saw him. "Just what we want for our soup stock!" she said. She popped Little Half Chick into a big pot of water.

"Oh, water!" he cried. "Have pity. Do not wet me like this!"

"When I was in trouble, you would not help me!" said the water. It bubbled all around him.

"Fire, please do not cook me!" begged Little Half Chick.

"When I was in trouble, you would not help me!" said the fire. It went on burning.

Just then, the wind blew by.

"Oh, wind, please come and help me," asked Little Half Chick.

"When I was in trouble, you would not help me," answered the wind. "But I will help you."

And the wind lifted Little Half Chick out of the pot. The wind carried him over the rooftops of Madrid. Then the wind left him on top of the highest steeple as a weathervane. There he stands on one leg, with his one wing drooping at his side, looking over the city with his one eye.

Anansi and Lizard

Once there was a king who had just one child, a lovely daughter. She grew into a beautiful young woman. And soon she was ready for marriage.

The king sent out messengers to make an announcement. Anyone who could guess the name of his daughter not only would marry her but also would be given half the kingdom. However, anyone who guessed the wrong name would have his head cut off!

Anansi, the spider man, had an idea. One night, he listened outside the princess's hut. He overheard one of her friends call her by her name, Ahoafe. Overjoyed, Anansi hurried home with his secret.

The next day on his way to the palace, Anansi met his friend, Lizard. Anansi told him his tremendous news but withheld the princess's name.

Lizard smiled. "How clever you are, Anansi!" he said. "But I think you should send a messenger ahead to announce that you're coming to see the king. Otherwise, he may not think you're worthy of respect – or his daughter's hand in marriage."

Lizard smiled even wider now.

"I'd be delighted to be your messenger, Anansi. But you had better tell me the princess's name. I don't want the king to chop my head off!"

"Well...all right. It's Ahoafe," whispered Anansi. "But remember to tell the king it was I, Anansi, who found this out."

Anansi watched as Lizard went off to the palace. Then Anansi hurried home to prepare himself for his wedding.

Inside the palace, Lizard told the king, "I have come to marry the princess. Her name is Ahoafe."

All around the kingdom, the news traveled fast. The princess was to be married. Anansi smiled to himself when he heard the news. He thought how wonderful he would look wearing a crown, with the princess beside him.

The next day, he waited to be summoned to his wedding. When no one came, he went to the market square. "Did you hear," someone said to him, "that the princess is marrying Lizard?"

"Nonsense," Anansi replied. "I only sent Lizard as my messenger. It is *I* who found out her name, not he."

Just then a procession came out of the palace gates and into the market square. On a litter decorated with jewels sat Lizard, wearing a crown on his head. Beside him was his new wife, Princess Ahoafe!

Anansi raised his eyes to the sky. He swore that if he ever saw Lizard again, he would tear him to pieces. And that is why, whenever you see a lizard, he is darting his eyes everywhere. He is watching out for Anansi, the spider man, who still hunts him to take his revenge.

The Tortoise
And the Hare

"I can run faster than any of you," boasted the hare. "But if anyone can beat me, I'll give the winner this shiny button. Who will try?"

The squirrel giggled. "Not I!"

"Oh, no, not me," said the fox.

"Weasel? Porcupine? Will nobody have a try?" asked the hare.

Just then, an old tortoise came plodding through the meadow.

The hare grinned slyly. "My dear Tortoise," he exclaimed, "you are just in time to have a chance to win this shiny button! Race me to the stone bridge!"

"Very well," said the tortoise, ignoring the laughter of the other animals.

The two lined up, side by side. Then one of the other animals said, "Ready! Set! Go!"

The hare leaped off to a lightning start. He was soon out of sight.

The tortoise, on the other hand, looked as if he was hardly even trying.

"Come on!" urged the watching animals. The tortoise slowly moved across the grass.

Meanwhile, the hare dashed along. Soon he reached the far side of the woods. He could see the stone bridge up ahead. It was a blazing hot day.

The hare thought to himself, *I'll stay in the cool woods for a while. The tortoise won't be here for hours.* He sat down by a fallen beech tree and leaned back

He had to get up and finish the race. He just couldn't let that old tortoise beat him.

While the hare was sleeping, the tortoise had plodded onward. Now he was within a few steps of the old stone bridge.

The hare gave a gigantic leap and bounded forward. But he was too late. The tortoise stepped onto the bridge. "The winner!" cried the animals.

The hare handed over his shiny button and walked slowly home. The tortoise just smiled and nodded. "Slow and steady wins the race," he said.

against its smooth trunk. Very soon he was fast asleep.

Sometime later, when the shadows were long, the hare woke up. *I must have been asleep for hours!* he thought.

How the Tortoise Got Its Shell

Long ago, the king of the gods decided to give a feast for all the animals. Invitations were sent out far and wide. All the animals in the kingdom accepted eagerly—except the tortoise.

"Why invite me? I don't want to go!" he said. "I can't dance. The food will be too rich for me, and I haven't got a thing to wear!"

So, on the day of the feast, the tortoise stayed home. Everyone else went to the palace.

The king of the gods spoke to each of his animal guests. When the feast was about to start, everyone sat down. But one chair was empty. Immediately, the king asked who had not come.

When he was told it was the tortoise, he sent for a messenger. The king told the messenger to go and get the missing guest.

In a little while, the messenger returned to the palace. He was dragging along a very annoyed tortoise who had been just about to settle down to a nice salad.

"Explain yourself!" ordered the king, looking very angry.

The tortoise faced him boldly. He said, "It was kind of you to invite me. But I would prefer to stay in my own little house. There's no place like home, you know."

The king of the gods went purple with rage. "Tell me," he said to the other gods, "what should I do with this ungrateful animal?"

"Simple!" cried the god of war. "Chop off his head!"

42

The tortoise trembled.

"No, no!" shouted the god of the sea. "I say he should be thrown to my sharks!"

"Oh!" said the tortoise with a gulp.

Then the goddess of wisdom spoke out. "I agree he should be punished for his bad manners. But we must think of a suitable way." She paused for a moment.

"I know," she said. "If he likes to stay at home so much, then let him be at home always. Let him carry his house around with him on his back."

The king of the gods nodded. That was the best idea. "So be it," he declared.

And that is why, to this very day, the tortoise is never without his shell.

The Lion
That Laughed

One summer, a huge circus came to town. Everybody went to the field where the big circus tent had been put up. At eight o'clock, the show began. All the seats were full.

The biggest attraction of the show was the Bravest Lion Tamer in the World. Everyone gasped with fear when a big cage was set up and a fierce-looking lion walked into it.

All of a sudden, before the cage door was properly shut, the lion gave a mighty roar. He leaped over the lion tamer and ran out of the cage. The lion ran around the outside of the ring. He stopped only to growl and flash his enormous teeth.

Some people screamed. Others fainted. Many people tried to run out of the tent. But the owner of the circus had closed all the entrances to prevent the lion from escaping into town.

"Please keep calm! Please keep calm!" shouted the lion tamer. "He won't hurt anyone. Just stay still!" But nobody believed him.

There were over a thousand people trapped in the big tent. They were all shouting and screaming. The lion paced up and down, growling and staring at the crowd.

"Get a rope and lasso him!" somebody shouted. "Fire the cannonball man at him!" cried a woman. But the man who was shot from the cannon did not want to be aimed at a lion!

Just then, a little boy in the front row shouted out, "The clowns! The clowns! Make him laugh! Make the lion weak with laughter!"

All the clowns came out and stood in front of the lion. Their legs shook with fear. They pretended the trembling was part of their act, and they walked with funny steps. They tripped over each

other and threw pies in each other's faces. They gave the best performance of their lives.

The lion began to smile and chuckle. After a few minutes, the lion was rolling on the ground, helpless with laughter.

The lion tamer came up with a collar and chain. He led the lion quietly away into the cage. The whole crowd cheered the clowns and the little boy for their bravery and cleverness.

45

The Ant and the Grasshopper

One hot summer's day, a grasshopper was dozing in the sun. He was thinking to himself how wonderful it was to do nothing but rest in the heat of the noonday sun.

Just then, a little ant came staggering by. She was carrying a large grain of barley on her back.

"Hello!" said the grasshopper. "Why are you so busy?"

"I am collecting food for my winter store. If you were smart, you'd do the same," said the ant.

"Not me!" said the grasshopper, chuckling. "You won't catch me working while the sun shines!"

And so the grasshopper lazed the summer away. When autumn came, he rushed around trying to

find enough food to last him for the whole winter. But by the time the first snow fell, his store was only half full.

"Oh, dear," he said to himself, "I hope I have enough food to last me through the winter."

But he did not. Spring was still several weeks away when the grasshopper found that there was nothing left in his store, not even a crumb. His eyes filled with tears. He was sure he would starve to death.

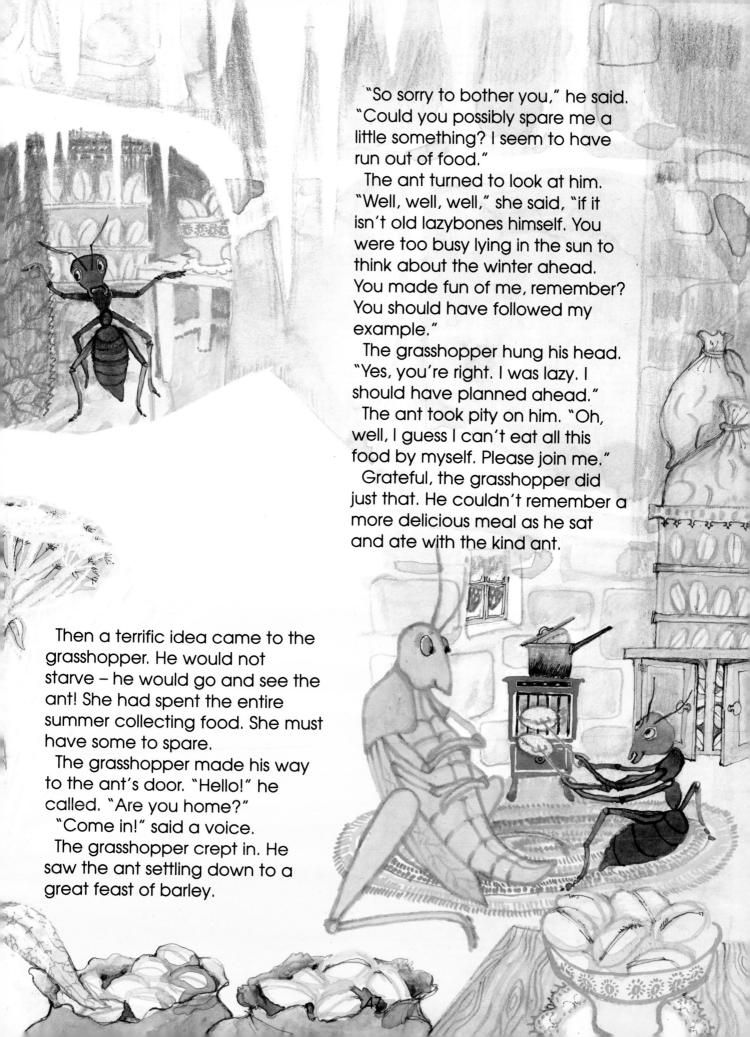

"So sorry to bother you," he said. "Could you possibly spare me a little something? I seem to have run out of food."

The ant turned to look at him. "Well, well, well," she said, "if it isn't old lazybones himself. You were too busy lying in the sun to think about the winter ahead. You made fun of me, remember? You should have followed my example."

The grasshopper hung his head. "Yes, you're right. I was lazy. I should have planned ahead."

The ant took pity on him. "Oh, well, I guess I can't eat all this food by myself. Please join me."

Grateful, the grasshopper did just that. He couldn't remember a more delicious meal as he sat and ate with the kind ant.

Then a terrific idea came to the grasshopper. He would not starve – he would go and see the ant! She had spent the entire summer collecting food. She must have some to spare.

The grasshopper made his way to the ant's door. "Hello!" he called. "Are you home?"

"Come in!" said a voice.

The grasshopper crept in. He saw the ant settling down to a great feast of barley.

Theseus and the Minotaur

Long, long ago, the king of Crete sent his only son to Athens in Greece. The boy was to run in the athletic games. The boy won many prizes at the games. But the Greek boys were so jealous that they killed him.

The king of Crete was very angry. He threatened to destroy Athens unless the king of Greece sent seven young men and seven young women to Crete every year. They were to be thrown to the terrible monster of Crete, the Minotaur. The Minotaur was half bull and half man.

The king of Greece was forced to agree. And so each year fourteen young people were sent to Crete and thrown to the Minotaur. None ever returned.

When the Greek king's son, Theseus, was old enough, he insisted that he be sent to Crete with the others of his age. "I know I can kill the Minotaur," he said. "Then Athens will be free of this terrible curse."

The king of Crete had a daughter named Ariadne. When she heard of the bravery of

48

she asked Theseus to take her with him back to Athens. Theseus gladly agreed to do this.

As Theseus entered the twisting passages the next day, he dropped one end of the thread at the entrance. He unwound the ball as he walked forward. He could smell the foul Minotaur and hear him roaring with hunger.

Suddenly, Theseus came upon the huge monster. They fought desperately. The Minotaur bellowed with rage as Theseus stayed clear of his vicious horns. Theseus finally thrust his sword into the beast and killed him.

Following the silken thread, Theseus found his way back out of the monster's lair. Then he made his way back to his ship with Ariadne and some other young Athenians who had been lost in the maze. Hoisting the sails, they set off for home, rejoicing that the monster was dead at last.

Theseus, she offered to help him. She told him that the Minotaur was kept deep inside a maze of twisting passages. Once inside, no one could find their way out.

Ariadne gave Theseus a ball of silken thread. She told him to leave one end at the entrance and to unwind the ball in his hand as he went. She also gave him a sword to hide in his tunic to use against the Minotaur. In return,

"Lord Mayor of London? Me? Surely not!" Dick said to himself. But he turned around and went back into London. There, he fell asleep on the doorstep of a rich merchant.

Dick was awakened by the merchant, who said he could live there if he worked in the kitchen. Dick agreed. He did all the jobs that nobody else wanted to do.

At night, Dick slept in an attic that was full of rats. So he saved up his money and one day bought a large cat. The cat chased away the rats. The cat slept at Dick's feet, keeping him warm.

Dick Whittington And His Cat

Many years ago, a boy from a small village in England decided to run away to London. His name was Dick Whittington. He had heard that the streets there were paved with gold.

But when Dick reached the city, he was bitterly disappointed. The streets were hard and dirty and full of garbage. "How will I ever make my fortune here?" he wondered aloud.

Dick walked back out of the city and into the countryside. He leaned up against a tree. He could hear church bells ringing in the city. They seemed to say:

> *Turn again, Whittington,*
> *Thou worthy citizen,*
> *Lord Mayor of London.*

One day, the merchant called all his servants before him. He said that he had a new ship that would be sailing on a long voyage. Everyone had to put something on the ship for good luck. Poor Dick had to send his cat because he had nothing else.

After many months, the ship landed at the port of a rich sultan. He invited the ship's captain to his palace for a feast. But when the captain arrived, there were hundreds of rats and mice running all over the food and wine.

"You need a cat!" the captain told the sultan. The captain sent a sailor back to the ship for Dick's cat.

The sultan laughed and clapped his hands as the cat chased all the mice and rats out of his palace. "What a splendid creature!" said the sultan. "I will give you two thousand gold pieces for him." The captain agreed.

When the ship returned to London, the captain gave Dick two bags full of gold. He said, "Now you have made your fortune."

Time went by. Dick married the merchant's daughter. The Lord Mayor of London himself came to the wedding. Ten years later, Dick was made Lord Mayor. But often he would walk in the countryside to hear the bells say:

Turn again, Whittington,
Thou worthy citizen,
Lord Mayor of London.

Rabbit Calls For Help

"It's nice having a friend," said Mole to Rabbit as they sat talking in the sun one day.

"Oh, it is!" said Rabbit. "Very useful, too, especially if you need help. In fact, I think I'd like Bull to be my friend."

"But *I'm* your friend!" said Mole, feeling hurt.

"Oh, yes," said Rabbit. "You are good for talking to and laughing with. But you are too small. When I need help, I want someone big and strong like Bull. He would be a very good friend to have. It would be nice shouting for him when I needed help."

"Well, suit yourself!" said Mole. He went off in a huff.

"What's the matter with him?" wondered Rabbit aloud. "Oh, well, I need something to eat."

Rabbit hopped along until he found a tiny garden. Another rabbit was already there, nibbling on some delicious lettuce leaves. Rabbit began to eat. He had never tasted anything so delicious in his whole life.

Rabbit had just started on his second lettuce when there was a great noise. People were shouting, dogs were barking, and doors were banging.

"Run for your life!" shouted the other rabbit.

Rabbit kicked up his heels and ran toward his burrow. He was so frightened and in such a hurry to get away that he ran into the wrong hole. The tunnel was too small. Halfway down, Rabbit got stuck. He could not move at all.

"Help!" cried Rabbit in a shrill, sharp voice. "Help!"

Mole heard him. He ran up to see what was the matter.

good! He's too big to get into this tunnel. You're just the right size! Please help me, Mole!"

So Mole dived into the tunnel. He dug around Rabbit with his strong front paws. Mole worked quickly. The soil flew out so fast that Rabbit was free in no time.

"I'm sorry, Mole. I was wrong," Rabbit said. "I'm glad I have you for a friend. We little animals should stick together."

And so the two good friends trotted off home together.

"Help!" cried Rabbit. "I'm stuck in this tunnel! Help!"

"If you want help," said Mole, "I'd better get Bull."

"No!" cried Rabbit. "He's no

The Lion And the Mouse

One day in Africa, a mouse was hurrying home. He was going so fast that he ran right into a sleeping lion. The lion awoke with a growl. He roughly curled his paw around the mouse.

"Ow! You're hurting me!" the mouse cried. "If you'll let me go, I'll repay you for your kindness!"

The lion shook with laughter. "How could a tiny creature like you help such a mighty beast as me?"

The lion thought it was amusing the way the mouse pleaded for his life. And besides, he wouldn't make a very big lunch. So the lion let him go.

"Thank you! I won't forget you," cried the mouse.

A few days later, some hunters came looking for wild animals.

They wanted to capture the animals and take them back to a zoo.

The hunters hung a big net from three trees. They tied a piece of meat so that it dangled just below the net. When an animal grabbed the meat, the net would fall on top of him and trap him.

One evening, the lion returned home in the darkness. He had made no kill that day. He was hungry for a juicy piece of meat. Just then, he smelled something delicious. It seemed to be somewhere among the trees.

When the lion finally found the meat, he pulled it down. That was when he realized that he had walked into a trap. The net fell down over him.

The lion kicked and clawed and roared. But it was no use. The more he struggled, the tighter the net pulled around him. After a

But the mouse got to work, gnawing through the net ropes with his sharp teeth. It took him a long time. But at last, he managed to make a hole in the net big enough for the lion to escape. The lion squeezed out of the net. It felt wonderful to be free again! He thanked the mouse and bounded off.

So the little mouse had done what he had promised to do — help the lion. One of nature's strongest and fiercest creatures had been saved by one of its smallest and weakest.

while, he stopped trying. He just lay there, moaning.

Not long afterward, the lion heard a tiny sound. It was the scampering of small feet near his head. He looked up and saw the mouse he had set free a few days ago.

"I've come to help you," said the mouse. "Just as I promised."

The lion groaned. "How can you help me? I'm caught in the net, can't you see? No one can help me now. Certainly not a little thing like you."

Hippo and the Pecking Bird

One very hot day in Africa, a large, fat hippopotamus was walking down a long and dusty road. He looked all around him, but there was no water anywhere.

"Oh, dear," said Hippo. "I am so hot and thirsty. If I don't find some water soon to cool me down, I will shrivel away until I am only half my size."

Just then, Hippo heard a pecking noise. He stopped and looked around, but he could not see anyone. "I must be hearing things. There is no one else here."

Then the noise came again. *Peck, peck.* And this time, there was a little voice, too. "I'm here on your back! Look!"

Hippo turned his head around as far as it would go. A little bird was perched on his back.

"I'm a pecking bird," the bird said. "I've been flying all day and all night. I'm very tired. If you will carry me on your back, I will show you where a river flows with lots of cool water."

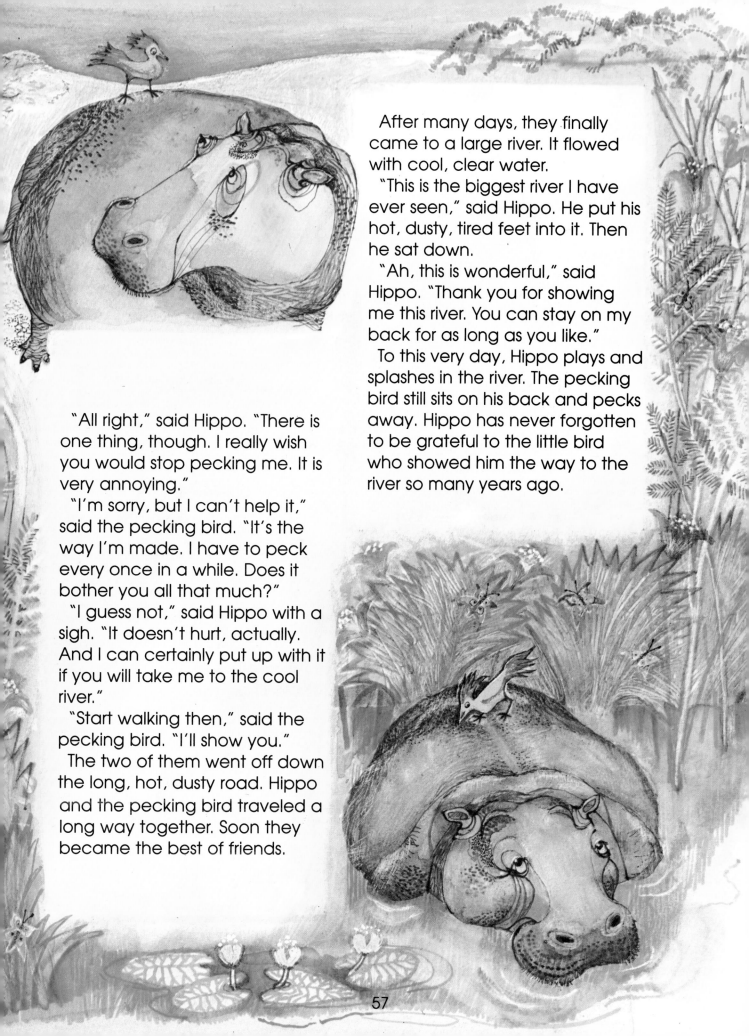

After many days, they finally came to a large river. It flowed with cool, clear water.

"This is the biggest river I have ever seen," said Hippo. He put his hot, dusty, tired feet into it. Then he sat down.

"Ah, this is wonderful," said Hippo. "Thank you for showing me this river. You can stay on my back for as long as you like."

To this very day, Hippo plays and splashes in the river. The pecking bird still sits on his back and pecks away. Hippo has never forgotten to be grateful to the little bird who showed him the way to the river so many years ago.

"All right," said Hippo. "There is one thing, though. I really wish you would stop pecking me. It is very annoying."

"I'm sorry, but I can't help it," said the pecking bird. "It's the way I'm made. I have to peck every once in a while. Does it bother you all that much?"

"I guess not," said Hippo with a sigh. "It doesn't hurt, actually. And I can certainly put up with it if you will take me to the cool river."

"Start walking then," said the pecking bird. "I'll show you."

The two of them went off down the long, hot, dusty road. Hippo and the pecking bird traveled a long way together. Soon they became the best of friends.

Puss in Boots

Once there was a clever cat who had a handsome but lazy young master. One day, the cat said, "Give me a pair of leather boots and a sack. I will catch something for our dinner."

His master spent his last money on a pair of boots for the cat. The cat put them on and left. After a very long time, he returned with a rabbit.

"Only one?" asked his master.

"I've been very busy," explained the cat. "I caught a lot more rabbits and took them to the palace. I told the king himself how they should be cooked for his supper."

The young man only laughed.

The next day, the cat went off on his own again. After a while, he came running up to his master. "Quick!" exclaimed the cat.

"Take off your clothes and dive into the river!" The master did as he was told.

The cat ran off and hid his master's shabby clothing. Just then, a carriage appeared. The king and the princess were inside. The cat went over to the carriage.

"This is my master, the Duke of Carabas, bathing in the river," said the cat, bowing to the king. "He is the one who sent you the fine rabbits yesterday. But a terrible thing has happened. Some robbers have stolen his clothing!"

The king was enraged. He sent a servant to the palace for some fine clothes. "You must come and dine with me at the palace."

"Yes," said the young man, too amazed to say anything else.

The cat said, "I will come back later and lead you all to my master's palace." Then the cat ran off.

He ran until he found a beautiful castle. He began to meow at the door. At last, it was opened by a very mean giant who lived there. The cat dashed inside.

"Can you work magic?" he asked the giant.

"Why, I can turn myself into a lion!" roared the giant.

"I don't suppose you can turn yourself into something small, like a mouse," said the cat, purring.

"I'll show you!" he bellowed.

The giant vanished, and a mouse stood in his place. The cat caught the mouse and gobbled him up. Then he ran to the king's palace. The cat asked that the carriage bring them all to the castle where the very mean giant once lived.

"This is the castle of my master," the cat told the king. The king was so impressed that he declared his daughter could marry this fine young man.

But the cat did not hear any of this. He was already fast asleep, curled up in a ball by the fire.

Three Billy Goats Gruff

Once there were three billy goats named Big, Middle, and Little Billy Goat Gruff. They lived beside a swiftly flowing river. On the other side of this river were fields of daisies that the three Billy Goats Gruff wanted to eat.

The only way to cross the river, however, was over an old stone bridge. They were too afraid to cross the bridge because underneath it lived a horrible old troll. And the troll's favorite snack was a billy goat!

One day, Little Billy Goat Gruff said, "I am going to cross over that bridge to the other side." And so he trotted onto the bridge.

Just when he was halfway across, the troll yelled out, "Who's crossing my bridge? This is my bridge, and I'm going to eat you for my dinner!"

"But I'm only a little, skinny goat," Little Billy Goat Gruff said. "Wait for my brother. He's much fatter than me. He'll taste much better."

"Well, all right," grumbled the troll. "But I hope he comes soon."

Little Billy Goat Gruff crossed into the fields of daisies and began to eat. His brothers were very jealous.

Middle Billy Goat Gruff decided he would try to cross the bridge, too. Just as he reached the middle, the troll roared, "Who's crossing my bridge? This is my bridge, and I'm going to eat you for my dinner!"

"Oh, no!" cried Middle Billy Goat Gruff. "Don't do that. You should wait for my brother. He'd make a delicious dinner for you!"

"All right," grumbled the troll, "but I hope he comes soon."

Middle Billy Goat Gruff ran across the bridge.

Big Billy Goat Gruff was all by himself, watching his brothers eat on the other side of the river. He decided he must cross the bridge even though he was afraid. He stamped his hoofs, shook his beard, and stepped firmly onto the bridge.

"Who's that crossing my bridge?" roared the angry troll.

"I've been waiting for you. You're going to be my dinner!" The horrible troll started to climb up the side of the bridge.

"Oh, no, I'm not!" shouted Big Billy Goat Gruff. He lowered his head and butted the troll with his horns. The troll toppled backward and fell into the water with a huge splash.

Big Billy Goat Gruff stepped proudly over the bridge. He ran into the fields full of daisies, where he began to eat and eat and eat with his brothers.

The Old Woman And Her Pig

An old woman went to the market to buy a pig. On the way home, she came to a fence. The pig would not go over it.

The woman saw a dog and said, "Dog! Bite pig! Pig won't go over the fence, and I won't get home tonight."

But the dog would not.

She saw a stick and said to it, "Stick! Beat dog!"

But the stick would not.

She met a fire and she said, "Fire! Burn stick!"

But the fire would not.

She saw some water and said, "Water! Quench fire!"

But the water would not.

She met an ox and she said, "Ox! Drink water!"

But the ox would not.

She saw a butcher and said, "Butcher! Kill ox!"

But the butcher would not.

The woman saw a rope and said, "Rope! Hang butcher!"

But the rope would not.

She saw a rat and said, "Rat! Gnaw rope!"

But the rat would not.

She saw a cat and said, "Cat! Kill rat! Rat won't gnaw rope. Rope won't hang butcher. Butcher won't kill ox. Ox won't drink water. Water won't quench fire. Fire won't burn stick. Stick won't beat dog. Dog won't bite pig. Pig won't go over the fence. And I won't get home tonight."

So the woman went to the haystack and brought the cow some hay.

As soon as the cow had eaten the hay, she gave the old woman the milk. The old woman took it in a saucer to the cat.

As soon as the cat had lapped up the milk, the cat began to kill the rat. The rat began to gnaw the rope. The rope began to

But the cat said to her, "If you will go to the cow and get me a saucer of milk, I will kill the rat."

So the woman went to the cow. But the cow said to her, "If you will go to the haystack and get me some hay, I will give you the milk."

hang the butcher. The butcher began to kill the ox. The ox began to drink the water. The water began to quench the fire. The fire began to burn the stick. The stick began to beat the dog. The dog began to bite the pig. The frightened pig jumped over the fence. And that's how the old woman got home that night.

Little Red Hen And the Grains Of Wheat

One day, Little Red Hen found some grains of wheat. "The farmer must have dropped them!" she said.

Just then, the cat, the farm dog, and the pig came by.

"I am going to plant these grains of wheat!" said Little Red Hen. "Would you like to help me?"

"Too tired!" said the dog, yawning.

"Can't be bothered!" said the cat, stretching out in the sun.

"Not today!" said the pig, who fell fast asleep.

"Then I shall have to plant them myself," said Little Red Hen.

By the end of the next summer, the grains had grown tall. Soon they were ready for harvesting.

"Will you help me harvest my wheat?" asked Little Red Hen.

"Too tired!" said the dog, yawning.

"Can't be bothered!" said the cat, stretching out in the sun.

"Not today!" said the pig, who fell fast asleep.

"Well!" said Little Red Hen. "I shall have to harvest it myself!"

After she harvested the wheat, Little Red Hen turned to the other animals again. "Now it's ready to be ground into flour. Will you help me carry it to the miller?"

"Too tired!" said the dog, yawning.

"Can't be bothered!" said the cat, stretching out in the sun.

"Not today!" said the pig, who fell fast asleep.

"I'll take it myself, then," sighed Little Red Hen. She dragged the heavy bag off to the mill.

"The flour is ready to be made into bread," she told the animals. "Will anyone help me bake it?"

"Too tired!" said the dog, yawning.

"Can't be bothered!" said the cat, stretching out in the sun.

"Not today!" said the pig, who fell fast asleep.

So, all by herself, Little Red Hen baked a fine, crusty loaf of bread. "Look what I have!" she cried.

"Ah, delicious!" the three other animals said.

"I suppose you are all too tired to help me eat it," said Little Red Hen.

"Tired?" said the dog in surprise.

"Not me!" said the cat.

"I'm never tired!" said the pig. "You can always count on me to help you."

"I don't think I need any help," said Little Red Hen. "I can eat it myself."

And she did – every single crumb!

Town Mouse and Country Mouse

In the corner of a field, a little brown mouse woke up one morning in her nest of hay. She decided to go and have some breakfast. Suddenly, she heard a shout.

"Hello! Is that you, Country Mouse?"

Country Mouse peered out of her nest and saw her cousin, Town Mouse.

"Please come in," she said. "I was just having some breakfast. Would you care for some barley? How about some wheat and a strawberry?"

Town Mouse shook his head. "Thank you, but no. That's too boring for me. You should come to the city. We'd have a feast there. I live in a big house, you know!"

Taking Country Mouse firmly by the paw, Town Mouse led her out of the quiet field. They walked along the roadside into the city.

Finally, they came to a long row of brick houses. They went through a gap under the wall. Soon they were in a large room full of chair legs and the smell of delicious cheese.

"Come on up!" called Town Mouse from the table. "But look out for the dishes. Oops!"

There was a crash of china. Just then, the door opened. A pair of big brown shoes clumped in. A voice said, "It's those rotten mice again!" The shoes went away, and the door was closed behind them.

"It's all right," said Town Mouse to his terrified cousin. "Here, try this cheddar cheese."

The cheese was the most wonderful flavor Country Mouse

had ever tasted in her whole life. It was much better than boring old wheat and barley.

Just as Country Mouse was about to take a second bite, the door opened again. Something black and furry was pushed into the room. It growled and hissed.

"The cat!" said Town Mouse with a squeak. "Run for your life!"

Across the floor, through the wall gap, down the road, and away from the city ran Country Mouse. She did not stop until she had reached her nest of hay in the corner of the field.

"Never again!" she said to herself, still panting from the long run. "What good is a feast if you have to risk your life to eat it? I'd rather have my wheat and barley and be able to eat them in peace!"

Little Lisa

One day, a girl named Little Lisa was skipping through the woods. She was wearing her best outfit. She had on a yellow dress, red shoes, a blue bonnet, and a snow-white apron. She carried a green umbrella. After a while, she saw some wild berries and wandered off to pick them. Soon Little Lisa had lost her way.

Suddenly, there was a terrible growl. Before her stood a bear.

"*Grr!*" he said. "I'm going to eat you up, little girl."

"Mr. Bear, I'll give you my white apron if you'll leave me alone," she said. "Try it on."

The bear was delighted with his new apron. "I am the most beautiful creature in the woods!" he said.

Little Lisa hurried on. Soon she met a wolf.

"*Grr!*" he said. "I'm going to eat you up, little girl."

"Mr. Wolf, I'll give you my blue bonnet if you'll leave me alone," Little Lisa said. "Try it on."

The wolf tried it on and ran off shouting, "I'm the most beautiful creature in the woods!"

Little Lisa went on a little farther. Soon she met a fox.

"*Grr!*" he said. "I'm going to eat you up, little girl."

"Mr. Fox, I'll give you my red shoes if you'll leave me alone. Please take them," Little Lisa said.

The fox snatched them from her and said, "I am the most beautiful creature in the woods!"

Little Lisa sat down and cried. She had lost most of her lovely new clothes. And she had lost her way home.

Just then, a rabbit found her. He said, "Don't cry, little girl. If you'll give me your green umbrella, I'll give you a ride home on my back. I know the way."

"You might as well have it, Mr. Rabbit," she said. "I've had to give everything else away today." Little Lisa climbed on the rabbit's back.

Suddenly, they heard a terrible roaring. The bear, the wolf, and the fox were fighting over who was the most beautiful creature in the woods. They had thrown off their new clothes.

Little Lisa ran over and picked up her clothing. She said, "Mr. Rabbit, please take me home while they are busy fighting. Hurry!"

The rabbit dashed through the woods to Little Lisa's house. When they arrived, the rabbit gave back her green umbrella. Little Lisa thanked the rabbit for his good deed and invited him in for supper.

Mouse Magic

Late one night in the old farmhouse, the farmer and his family were fast asleep. But in the kitchen a very odd argument broke out. The floorboards groaned, "All day long, big heavy feet trample all over us."

"Well," said the iron poker, "I have to put up with being roasted in the fire all day!"

"If I weren't burning all day," hissed the fire, "everyone would have a cold dinner!"

"Be quiet, all of you!" yelled the clock. "None of you work as hard as I do, all day, all night, *tick tock*.

I can't stand it anymore! It's driving me crazy!"

The clock's hands began to whirl around its face. A strange noise came from its insides. Then suddenly, it fell silent.

"The clock just needs a rest," said the iron poker. "And with a clock that doesn't work, no one will know when to get up. We'll all get a rest!"

Now a little mouse was listening to this conversation. The mouse suddenly was alarmed. With no clock, there would be no breakfast time. Would there be no more lunches and suppers? No more scraps from the kitchen table? He ran to tell the other mice.

"I know the answer," said the oldest mouse. "We need Dusty Dan. He is a very old clock who lives at the top of the house. He doesn't work anymore because no one winds him up. If we could get him working again, everyone in the house would know the time."

So all the mice crept up the stairs to the top landing. There stood Dusty Dan. The mice began cleaning and polishing him inside and out.

Poor old Dusty Dan had not received so much attention in years. Finally, by morning, he was working beautifully. He kept exact time.

At 7 A.M., the farmer and his wife were awakened by Dusty Dan's beautiful chimes.

"Why, that's Dusty Dan!" said the farmer. "That clock hasn't chimed for years. I'd forgotten it was there."

"It's a lovely sound to wake up to," said the farmer's wife. "But what made it chime after all these years?"

"Must be magic," said the farmer.

He and his wife went down to breakfast. They didn't notice the pitter-patter of mice feet on the stairs behind them.

The Frog Prince

One day, a beautiful princess was tossing a golden ball at the edge of a pond. Unfortunately, she threw it too far. It splashed down deep into the pond. The princess thought it was gone forever. She began to cry.

"Don't cry, Princess," a voice said. She looked up and saw a large frog staring at her. "I can get it for you," said the frog. "But will you let me be your companion if I do?"

"I promise!" said the princess.

The frog dived into the water and brought the golden ball back up to the surface. He threw it to the princess. She grabbed it and, without even saying "thank you," ran back to the palace. *How stupid to think I would let a frog be my companion!* she thought to herself.

The next day during a large feast at the palace, there was a knock at the door. A voice said, "Sweet princess, open the door. Have you forgotten your promise?"

"What promise?" the king asked his daughter. The princess explained how a frog had done her a favor.

The king was very angry when he heard how the princess had run away and broken her promise. "You must always keep a promise, even to a frog. Go and let him in!" the king commanded.

The princess opened the door. The frog hopped in and followed her to her seat.

"Lift me up to the table," he croaked. "Put your gold plate nearer, so I can reach it. And give me a drink from your crystal goblet." When she had done these things, the frog said, "I am tired. Where is your bed?"

The princess began to cry at the thought of a horrible frog in her nice, clean bed. The frog was already hopping up the stairs.

"I want to sleep on your silk pillow. Put me there, or I'll tell your father that you refused," said the frog.

The princess took her silk pillow and placed it outside her bedroom door. There, the frog slept all night.

When the princess woke up the next morning, she walked to the door and opened it. Standing on the silk pillow before her was a tall, handsome prince. He was smiling.

"Thank you, Princess," he said. "By keeping your promise, you have broken the spell. A wicked witch had turned me into a frog," he said. "Will you marry me?"

The princess agreed to marry the Frog Prince. She lived happily in his castle – and was always sure to be kind to frogs.

The Fox
And the Stork

It was at the animals' midsummer ball that the stork first met the fox. They danced together several times. After the last waltz, the fox said, "Lovely lady, I would be greatly honored if you would have dinner with me next Tuesday."

The stork said she would be happy to accept his invitation. And when the evening arrived, she set off for the fox's house.

"I am so pleased to see you," said the fox as he opened the door. "Do come in!"

"Thank you," said the stork. *What a delightful friend I have found*, she thought. *And such a gentleman.*

"I have prepared some lettuce soup for our dinner," said the fox. "Would you care to try some?"

"Oh, yes, please," said the stork eagerly. By this time, she was very hungry.

The stork dipped her beak into the soup. But the bowl was so shallow that she could not manage to sip more than a tiny taste. The fox was eating merrily away.

"Not hungry?" he asked, grinning. "Never mind. I'll eat it."

The stork was quite offended. The fox's manners were terrible! It seemed that he had chosen the soup on purpose to make her feel uncomfortable.

"I would be glad if you would dine with *me* next week," she said politely. "I would like to return your kindness."

"Why, yes," said the fox.

A week went by. Now it was time for the fox to visit the stork. She let him in as soon as he arrived.

The fox followed the stork into the dining room. Then he sniffed the air. "Ah, stew, if I am not mistaken. I can hardly wait."

"Please sit down," said the stork, "and allow me to serve you." She brought the stew in two tall, slim jugs. "Here we are," she said.

The fox stared in dismay.

"Do start," said the stork. She used her long beak to reach the bottom of the jug.

"I can't reach it with my mouth!" he said.

"Oh, dear, then I shall have to eat it myself," said the stork. "Kindly pass it to me."

The fox stood up. "Madame, I think you are most unpleasant to treat me this way. If this is your idea of how to treat a dinner guest, I shall leave."

The stork merely smiled. "As you wish, my dear sir," she answered. "You set the example. You really shouldn't complain when I follow it."

The Cat and
The Painter

One night, a lonely old cat was wearily walking down the street. It was pouring rain, and the cat was hoping to beg for some food.

Walking along, the cat noticed a hole in the back door of a house. He climbed through it and went up a dark staircase. At the top, he walked into a room. A young man was there.

"I'm sorry to drop in on you like this," said the cat. "But I was hoping you could feed me."

"All right," replied the young man. "But I am poor myself, so don't expect much. I am a struggling painter, and I am as poor as you."

The old cat looked around the studio. There were paintings on the wall, and brushes and pens and pencils everywhere. The young man knew the room was messy. But to the old cat, it was a palace.

The painter gave the cat some milk and bread. He also showed the cat a warm spot by the stove. The cat, purring softly, fell asleep.

It rained all the next day. Few people went to the market where the painter sold his work.

"That's enough!" he said when he returned. "I couldn't sell a single painting. I have no money left. One of us will have to go."

"Please don't give up," said the cat. "Let me stay. We will not go hungry. You'll see."

Then the cat fell asleep. He dreamed that the painter sold a painting. While he was sleeping, the cat spoke aloud. "Gone!" he said. "One is bought."

The painter heard the cat and wondered what he meant.

On the next market day, the painter returned early. He was carrying a bag full of groceries.

"You see, I told you not to give up," said the cat. "Today you sold one painting. Next time, you'll sell more."

He took ten cans of cat food out of a bag. Then he pulled out a bright red collar with a bell on it.

"Will you wear this and stay with me forever?" the painter asked.

"I think I will," said the old cat. "Life has taken a turn for the better since we met each other. You will paint and I will sit by the stove and keep you company."

The cat fell asleep and dreamed that the painter sold ten paintings. "Good!" he said in his sleep. "All ten paintings have been bought." Again, the painter heard the cat speak but did not understand.

The next market day came. When the painter returned, he was singing happily. The cat knew his dream had come true.

"I've sold ten paintings today!" cried the painter. "Ten! And look what I've bought!"

Paul Bunyan and John McGrew

It was the first day of the spring thaw. A young lumberjack named John McGrew decided to challenge Paul Bunyan to a fight. Paul Bunyan was considered the strongest lumberjack in the world.

That morning, Paul Bunyan woke up and yawned, causing four giant pine trees outside to crash to the ground. Paul stepped out of his huge bed and stretched. Far to the north, a great sheet of ice cracked under the strain.

Suddenly, Paul thought he heard someone shout, "Paul Bunyan, I've come to fight you!"

He went out of his cabin, but the only person he could see was young John McGrew. "There's John McGrew," Paul said to himself. "Perhaps he's come to ask for a job."

Paul bent down and playfully picked up a pair of oxen, then put them down. John McGrew rubbed his eyes in amazement. Paul Bunyan had lifted the two oxen as if they were two mice!

As Paul Bunyan reached the edge of the field, Babe, the Blue Ox, came by. Babe was Paul Bunyan's pet. Babe was a big, strong, blue ox.

John was delighted. They went off together to Sam Sourdough's Cook House. They sat down to an enormous meal and washed it down with gallons of hot coffee.

"You know," said Paul to Sam and John, "I could have sworn I heard someone yelling before breakfast. The person said, 'Paul Bunyan, I've come to fight you!'"

"Nah!" said Sam. "That was just your stomach rumbling. Don't I always tell you not to work before breakfast?"

John stood and watched as Paul hitched Babe up to the plow. In less than half an hour, they had plowed forty fields.

John looked at Paul Bunyan and then at Babe, the Blue Ox. John remembered what his grandmother had always told him: "John, if you can't beat 'em, join 'em!" *Maybe she was right!* he thought.

John shouted across the field, "Mr. Bunyan, sir, could you use a tough lumberjack?"

Paul squinted over to where the voice had come from. "John McGrew, I've heard you're a real good worker. I sure could use you. Want some breakfast first?"

Now Paul Bunyan sleeps late in the morning. It is John McGrew who gets up early and hitches Babe, the Blue Ox, to the plow. They work until forty fields are plowed. Then John wakes Paul up, and the two head over to the cook house for pancakes and maple syrup.

Buffalo and Porcupine

One evening at the local water hole, Buffalo spoke to his neighbor, Porcupine.

"I'm tired of this place," said Buffalo. "The time has come for me to leave. I have decided I am going to go tomorrow morning."

Porcupine was sorry to hear this. Even though Buffalo was sometimes very rude to Porcupine, he was a very useful neighbor to have. Buffalo always knew when a storm was coming. He knew where there was fresh grass. So, overlooking past insults, Porcupine asked, "May I come with you?"

"You," answered Buffalo with a snort, "with short legs like that! You would never keep up with me."

Despite this insult, Porcupine was determined to go.

The next morning, Buffalo was up at dawn. He traveled many miles. Buffalo did not know that Porcupine was following far behind him.

A few days later, a hungry lion saw Buffalo. The lion decided to attack him. After a long chase, Buffalo plunged into a river. The lion, not wanting to get wet, gave up and went home.

Meanwhile, Porcupine had reached the river himself. He was

Buffalo was so flattered that he agreed to take Porcupine across. So, with Porcupine safely on his back, Buffalo started to swim across the river.

Halfway across, Porcupine took one of his quills and pricked Buffalo with it.

"Ouch!" cried Buffalo. "Why did you do that?"

"I'm showing you that I'm not a worthless little creature with short legs. Now you see why no lion would dare attack me!"

When they reached the other side, Porcupine got off. Buffalo looked at the quills on Porcupine's back. Why had he never noticed before how many quills Porcupine had?

Maybe old friends were the best friends after all. Buffalo and Porcupine agreed that they would look for a new home together. And Buffalo promised never to insult Porcupine again.

wondering how to get across it. Buffalo saw him and said, "What are *you* doing here?"

"Looking for a new home with you," said Porcupine. "Despite my short legs, I have followed you all this way. Now, would you please be so kind as to carry me across this river on your back? I am only a poor small creature with stumpy legs. I cannot even swim."

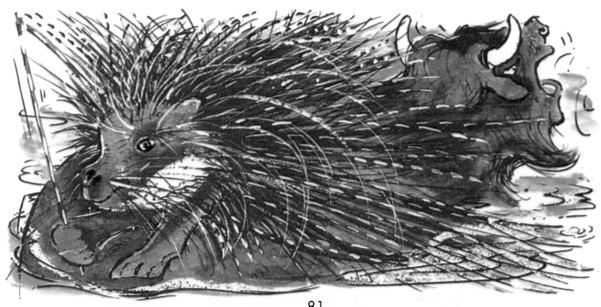

The Ugly Duckling

It was a beautiful summer's day. In the middle of the farmyard, a mother duck was sitting with her newly hatched ducklings. They were all waiting for one last egg to hatch.

At last, the egg burst open. The baby bird struggled out. He was very large and ugly with straggly gray feathers.

"None of my other ducklings looks like that," said the mother duck. "Perhaps he is a turkey. Well, there is one way to find out. Turkeys can't swim."

Soon the mother took her ducklings to the water. They all jumped in and began to swim. The large, ugly duckling swam the best of all.

She took her flock back up to the farmyard. All the other ducks ran up to the ugly duckling and pulled his feathers. A big turkey strutted up and made gobbling noises in his face. The poor duckling was terrified. Even his brothers and sisters were cruel to him. The ugly duckling decided to go off on his own. He came to a marsh where he met a pair of geese.

"You're a strange-looking fellow," they said. "But you can fly with us if you want."

Just then, there was a terrible noise of gunshot. The two geese fell over dead. The duckling saw two hunters among the trees. A dog rushed in to pick up the

dead geese. The dog saw the ugly duckling but did not touch him.

"Thank goodness I'm so ugly," the duckling said softly to himself. "The dog doesn't even want to bite me."

Soon fall came. The ugly duckling sheltered himself from the cold wind in some bushes.

One evening, a whole flock of swans passed overhead. The ugly duckling watched with envy as they spread their white wings and flew.

At last, spring came. The ugly duckling found that his wings had grown very large and strong. He flew into the sky and landed in a large park. He saw three swans swimming in the distance. The ugly duckling was so lonely that he flew over to meet them. He was expecting them to chase him off.

But what was this he saw in the clear water? No ugly, gray bird looked back at him! All he saw was a beautiful, white swan. The ugly duckling realized that it was himself. He had become a swan!

The other swans swam over to him. They stroked his feathers gently with their beaks to welcome him to their flock.

The Clever Monkey

An elephant was wandering along a river in the jungle. He came upon a loaf of bread.

"Mmm," he murmured as he sniffed. "This smells good."

He was about to put the loaf into his mouth when an alligator appeared. The alligator snapped at the bread, missing by an inch.

"Hey!" trumpeted the elephant. "I saw it first!"

"You can't prove it," said the alligator. "I'm going to eat the loaf and your nose, too, if it gets in my way." The alligator hissed and flashed his teeth.

"Don't threaten me, you reptile!" roared the elephant. "I could squash you with one footstep!"

A little monkey nearby heard the argument. He also wanted some of the loaf of bread. He thought, *I can't use fierceness or size to fight for the bread. But I can use my wits.*

The monkey spoke to the quarreling pair. "Gentlemen, I see you cannot decide who should have this bread. The fairest way to settle this is to hold three contests. We will each choose the kind of contest we want."

"I choose a contest to see who is the strongest!" bellowed the elephant. With that, he heaved a tree out of the ground.

"I choose a contest to see who can swim the fastest across the

"And now my contest is to find out who's the cleverest," said the monkey.

"How do we do that?" asked the elephant.

"It's easy," answered the monkey. "I am the cleverest for settling an argument that you could not do for yourselves. So the third piece is for me!"

While the elephant and the alligator tried to figure it all out, the monkey swung himself up into the treetops. There he sat, enjoying his part of the prize in peace.

river and back!" said the alligator with a sneer. He sped to the far side of the river and was back in a flash.

"You have each won a contest," said the monkey. "I will break off an equal piece of bread for each of you. I will save a third piece for the winner of the third contest." The two competitors gobbled down their share.

Baron Munchausen And the Bear

Traveling by horse and cart, Baron Munchausen was passing by an army camp one morning. The guard on duty said the camp was expecting a visit from a general. Everything had to be spick-and-span and ready for action.

"Splendid!" said Baron Munchausen, who went on his way.

On the road, he met a peasant who had been gathering nuts for the winter. The baron decided to help him. He left the horse and cart in a clearing, and the two went into the woods with more sacks to fill.

When they came back, they saw something horrible. A wild bear had climbed into the cart! The bear was busy eating the nuts the peasant had already gathered.

"Shoo!" cried the peasant.

The horse, thinking the command was for him, leaped forward and galloped through the woods. The bear began to roar loudly. The poor horse went crazy with terror and ran even faster. Baron Munchausen tried to catch them.

A short while later, back at the army camp, a soldier suddenly shouted. He pointed at a cloud of dust approaching at a great speed along the road. "Here comes the general!" the soldier said.

All the soldiers stood at attention. The crowd pressed forward. The band struck up the national anthem. People waved flags and shouted, "Long live the general!"

Into the middle of all this clattered the horse and cart. The bear was snarling in anger among the sacks.

Baron Munchausen, who was a very fast runner, arrived at the camp almost at the same time. He ran to the cart and grabbed the bear by his tail. The bear was so surprised that he fell off the cart and broke his neck.

The music stopped. The crowd was completely silent. At last, the mayor stepped forward. He looked at the bear and said angrily, "Baron Munchausen! This is not the general!"

"No, it isn't," agreed the baron. "It is a dead bear. Poor creature. And these," he added, pointing to the sacks, "are nuts."

When the general arrived, he wanted to know what had happened. "Who can tell me the bare facts here?" he asked.

Baron Munchausen stepped forward. He was smiling slightly. "I can tell you the *bear* facts, General." And so he did.

The Bear and The Travelers

Two young men named Richard and Bill set out on a journey. Then one evening, Richard tripped over a rock and fell to the ground. He yelled out in pain. "I think I've sprained my ankle," he said.

Bill helped Richard up and gave him his shoulder to lean on. "We must get to safety before dark," said Bill, "or we may be attacked by bears."

Poor Richard was in a lot of pain, but he struggled on.

The two were making their way through the woods when suddenly they heard a sound. Something was coming toward them through the trees! They could hear it dragging its big, heavy feet through the fallen leaves.

"A bear!" yelled Bill. He let go of Richard, who sank to the ground. Then Bill raced to the nearest tree and scrambled up it.

Richard watched the bear come closer. He was sure that it would kill him. Then he remembered something his grandfather had told him when he was a little boy: "A bear will never hurt you if you lie still."

"What?" said Bill, getting red in the face.

Richard put up a hand to stop him. "If you were really my friend," he declared, "you wouldn't have left me to face the bear alone."

Looking around, Richard saw a good-sized stick lying on the ground nearby. "Now," he said, reaching for the stick to help him walk, "I'll use this the rest of the way. It will be a better friend to me than you were."

Richard pretended to be dead. He lay flat and held his breath. The bear was now very close to him.

It seemed that Richard stayed frozen with terror for hours. The bear sniffed at his head and walked around him a few times. Then, the bear gave up and wandered off through the woods.

Bill climbed down from the tree. "Gosh!" he said. "That was a close call! You know, it looked as if that bear were whispering in your ear. Did it say anything to you?"

Richard sat up and smiled to himself. "It said," he answered slowly, "that I should never travel with friends who run away and leave me as soon as danger appears."

Cuthbert Crocodile

Cuthbert Crocodile lived in a nice, swampy pond in a zoo. He had everything he could possibly want. Cuthbert knew he should be happy. He *would* have been happy except for one thing. He could not clean his teeth.

The trouble with crocodiles is that they have very long mouths. It would take a very long toothbrush to reach each tooth properly. Then, it would require some skill to steer around every single tooth. And Cuthbert didn't even have a toothbrush!

He grew sadder and sadder. His teeth felt dirtier and dirtier. He was shy when people came to see him at the zoo.

"I want to see his teeth!" a little boy shouted one day. "Where are his teeth?"

Cuthbert clamped his mouth shut. He was too ashamed to show his dirty teeth.

One day, Cuthbert heard a noise near his pond. Suddenly, he saw a terrified mouse being chased by a big cat.

Cuthbert was already upset about his teeth, but he was furious that someone would invade his privacy. He lunged out of the water, opened his long

mouth, and *clunk*! He snapped his jaws shut around the mouse. The cat ran away in fright.

That will teach them! Cuthbert thought. But soon he felt a knocking on his teeth. He opened his mouth. A squeaky voice said, "Excuse me, but what dirty teeth you have."

Cuthbert was angrier than ever! He shut his mouth with a very loud snap.

"But it's true!" the voice said from inside. "If you like, I could climb in here with a toothbrush and toothpaste and brush your teeth for you. In return, you could protect me from that mean cat."

Cuthbert's jaw dropped open, and a tiny mouse jumped out.

"Could you really?" he asked.

"No problem," said the mouse. "But you have to promise not to swallow me."

"Of course I wouldn't swallow you!" roared Cuthbert. "If you clean my teeth, I will be happy to protect you. You can live here with me."

The mouse was delighted. He got right down to work that same day.

Now, Cuthbert flashes his shiny teeth all day and scares everyone-except, of course, the mouse. And every night he dreams of peppermint toothpaste.

91

The Fox and the Little Red Hen

Once upon a time, a little red hen lived in a house by herself in the woods. Over the hill among some rocks lived a sly, crafty fox. The fox lay awake nights, thinking how he could catch the little red hen. He wanted to carry her home to cook for his supper.

But this clever little red hen was very careful. She never went far from her house without locking the door and putting the key in her pocket. The fox watched and prowled until he grew thin and pale. But he could find no way to catch the little red hen.

At last, the fox had an idea. One morning, he put a big bag over his shoulder and said to his mother, "Have the pot boiling when I come home. I'll bring the little red hen for supper."

Away the fox went through the woods and over the hill to where the little red hen lived in her cozy little house. Just as he got there, the little red hen came out to collect sticks for her fire. That's when the fox slipped unseen into the house. He hid behind the door.

Soon, the little red hen came inside. She closed the door, locked it, and put the key in her pocket. When she saw the fox, she dropped her sticks and flew up onto the rafter under the roof.

"Ah," said the fox, "I'll soon

bring you down." He began to spin around and around, faster and faster, chasing after his big, bushy tail. The little red hen looked at him until she got dizzy and fell to the floor. The fox grabbed her, put her into his bag, and started for home.

Over the hill and through the woods he went with the little red hen tied tightly in the bag. After a while, the fox lay down to rest. As the fox slept, the smart little red hen put her hand in her pocket and took out a bright, shiny pair of scissors. She snipped a hole in the bag and quietly slipped out. Picking up a big stone, the little red hen dropped it into the bag and ran home as fast as her legs could carry her.

Not long afterward, the fox woke up and started walking again with his bag over his shoulder. "My, how heavy the little red hen is," said the fox. "What a nice meal I shall have!"

His mother was standing at the door of his home, waiting for him. "Mother," the fox asked, "do you have the pot boiling?"

"Yes, I do," she replied. "Do you have the little red hen?"

"Right here in my bag. Lift the lid of the pot and let me put her in," said the fox.

The fox untied the bag and held it over the boiling water. Splash! The heavy stone fell into the boiling water.

"That hen tricked me!" said the fox.

"She's smarter than you," said his mother. "Your dinner tonight will be this stone soup. Maybe then you will remember you're not such a sly fox after all."

How Jack Went to Seek His Fortune

Once upon a time, there was a boy named Jack. One morning, he started to go and seek his fortune. He had not gone very far before he met a cat.

"Where are you going, Jack?" asked the cat.

"I am going to seek my fortune."

"May I go with you?"

"Yes," said Jack. "The more, the merrier."

And off the two went. They traveled a little farther and soon met a dog.

"Where are you going, Jack?" asked the dog.

"I'm going to seek my fortune."

"May I go with you?"

"Yes," said Jack. "The more, the merrier."

And off the three went. They traveled just a little farther before they met a goat.

"Where are you going, Jack?" asked the goat.

"I am going to seek my fortune."

"May I go with you?"

"Yes," said Jack. "The more, the merrier."

And off the four went. They traveled a little farther and soon met a bull.

"Where are you going, Jack?" asked the bull.

"I am going to seek my fortune."

"May I go with you?"

"Yes," said Jack. "The more, the merrier."

And off the five went. They traveled a little farther before they met a rooster.

"Where are you going, Jack?" asked the rooster.

"I am going to seek my fortune."

"May I go with you?"

"Yes," said Jack. "The more, the merrier."

And off the six went. They traveled until it was almost dark. They began to look for a place to spend the night.

About this time, they came in sight of a house. Jack told them to be quiet while he went and looked in a window. To his surprise, there were robbers counting over their money.

Jack had an idea. He went back and told the animals to wait until he gave the word and then to make as much noise as they

94

could. When they all were ready, Jack gave the word.

The cat meowed, the dog barked, the goat bleated, the bull roared, and the rooster crowed. All together, they made such an awful noise that it frightened away all the robbers. The animals then went into the house and rested.

Jack was afraid the robbers would come back during the night, so he thought of another plan. He put the cat in the rocking chair, the dog under the table, the goat upstairs, and the bull in the cellar. The rooster flew onto the roof. At last, Jack went to bed.

Later that night, the robbers saw that the house was dark. They sent one man back to the house to look for their money. Before long, he came running out of the house, making quite a noise. It awoke Jack, who hurried downstairs, saw the man, and followed him. With Jack listening

from a nearby bush, the terrified robber joined the others and told them his story.

"I went back to the house," he said, "and went in. But it was very dark. I tried to sit down in the rocking chair, but it seemed there was someone knitting. Sharp knitting needles stuck into me!"

Jack knew it was the cat's sharp claws.

"I found my way to the table to look for the money. A shoemaker must have been under the table, for he stuck some sort of pointed tool into my leg."

Jack knew it was one of the dog's sharp teeth.

"I was getting frightened and tried to go upstairs. But then someone knocked me down."

Jack knew the man had been butted by the goat's horns.

"So I started to go down to the cellar. There was someone down there pounding nails. Suddenly, I was knocked up the stairs with his hammer."

Jack knew it was the bull's powerful head.

"But I shouldn't have been all that frightened if it hadn't been for that little fellow on top of the roof. He seemed to be saying, 'Kill him, whatever you do! Kill him, whatever you do!' When I heard that, out the door I ran!"

Jack knew it was the rooster crowing "cock-a-doodle-do." Trying not to laugh out loud, he hurried back to the house. There, he told all the animals the story he had just heard.